GRIM LOV

Lilith Leana

Acknowledgement

A big thank you to my husband for always believing in me and never making me feel like I couldn't do it.

Cover art

Cover art from Depositphoto

Cover design

Lilith Leana with Canva

Brief Summary

The Frog Prince

What if the Swan Princess kissed the Frog Prince, and they helped each other to break their curse?

Odette has been cursed by an evil wizard over a decade ago. She spends her days as a swan, and changes back to human during the night. When she kisses a frog, he turns in a handsome prince who wants to help her break her curse.

Henry has been hopping around as a frog for more than two decades. When he gets kissed by a beautiful maiden princess, the curse is broken. Now he wants to do anything possible to help her break her curse, even if it means giving her all of him.

The Genie

What if Aladdin didn't find the Magic Lamp but Princess Jasmine did?

Princess Jasmine is determined to help her people. When she finds a magic lamp, and gets three wishes she can finally do so.

The Genie has been trapped in his lamp for an eternity. When he is roused by a beautiful princess to help her save her land, he will do anything in his power to obey her, even if her last wish asks more of him than he has ever given anyone.

Peter & Pan

What if Peter & Pan grew up and revisited Wendy?

Wendy has grown up, and is living in London when she wakes up and finds her first love on her terrace asking for her help.

Peter needs Wendy's help to find his shadow again. Pan wants to stay in London and grow old with Wendy.

The Fae Guardian

What if Cinderella didn't have a Fairy Godmother, but a Fae Guardian?

Ella meets her Fae Guardian in the woods after she runs away from her step-family. He promises to grant all her wishes, but there is one wish that might ask too much of him.

Varden has been Ella's Fae Guardian since she was born. He always kept an eye out on her, never realizing how badly her stepfamily treated her until they go too far, and hurt her. He will do everything in his power to make Ella happy, even if it means giving her his heart.

The Dragon

What if Rapunzel was guarded by a Dragon who fell in love with her, and helped her get out of her tower?

Rapunzel has lived in her tower for all her life, never daring to dream of a life outside of it. But when her dragon offers her an opportunity, she can't turn it down.

Tanwen has been cursed to be a dragon and guard the witch's tower. He watches Rapunzel grow up into a beautiful woman, and is determined to help her free herself from the tower. He only hopes that she will want to carry his curse to do so.

READER ADVISORY: THIS story contains explicit sex scenes.

Grim Lovers 2 is a collection of five previously published standalone short erotic stories.

It is filled with your favorite fairytale retellings. Explicit sex scenes, standalone, no cheating or cliffhangers.

The Frog Prince

What if the Swan Princess kissed the Frog Prince, and they helped each other to break their curse?

I WAS CRAVING FROG. I hated how I needed to eat foul creatures when I was in Swan form to be able to sustain myself. I had to be strong enough to turn human at sunset each night, or I would remain a Swan forever.

A frog jumped up on a stone, to bask in the evening sun, unbeknown he would be my dinner tonight. I flew up high, letting my wings take me up in the sky. After assessing the distance, I swooped down, aiming for the frog. Right before I could catch it with my beak, it made a strange sound. It was just enough to distract me, so it could jump off the rock, into the safety of the waters.

With a sigh I let it go, gracefully landing on the water. I folded my wings back up my body and paddled the last bit of distance to my shore, where I could catch the last of the evening sun.

I could feel the transformation take place, and from one moment to the next, I was standing on the shore on my human legs. Stretching out my arms, I tried to catch the last of the sun before it was gone, leaving me alone in the night.

The frog I had almost eaten, jumped up at the shore next to me, making that strange sound again. It sounded like something between a ribbit and a human laugh. Crouching down, I smiled at it, giving it a soft pat on its head.

"Sorry, I almost ate you."

I could hunt again in the morning, and it felt nice having someone next to me in the night. The other animals usually steered clear of me in my human form, but for some reason, this frog didn't seem to mind. It made that same curious sound again, that didn't seem like a normal noise a frog should make. I bent over,

4

getting a better look at it. The green skin gleamed in the moonlight, and the black specks made it camouflage easily in the water. The frog looked back at me with strange brown eyes that seemed to have more intelligence behind them than I would suspect. As I cocked my head to the side to study it closer, it mirrored my movements.

I got on my knees so I could bend lower to study it, not caring about the dirt that got on my white dress. Suddenly I got the undeniable urge to kiss it. I tried to banish the thought, but it somehow circled back into my mind each time I looked into its eyes. It wasn't as if I had anything better to do and what harm could it do?

"I'm not going to eat you," I said in a soothing voice, as I lowered my head.

I puckered my lips, and the frog made an excited sound. Taking that as much consent as I could, I gave it a gentle kiss on the top of its head. I could feel a zing pass through me, and sparks flew through the air. Backing up, I landed on my butt, as I watched in amazement at the lights before me.

Suddenly there was a man standing where the frog had been. A very handsome, and naked man. It had been ages since I had seen another human, and I took in his form with pleasure. He had amazingly muscular legs, a very impressive cock, and a flat stomach. My eyes reached higher, and I could see the same brown eyes that the frog had, staring back at me. His face had a classically handsome look, a strong jaw, supple lips, and beautiful brown curls that I wanted to run my hands through.

"Thank you," he said, with a smile that transformed his face, and made him incredibly handsome. He ducked down and swooped me up in a hug. "Thank you so much," he said as he whirled me around in the air.

A laugh escaped me for the first time in a decade. On instinct, I grabbed his shoulders, as he whirled me around. He put me down, gently grasping my face, his fingers soft on my cheeks. I almost closed my eyes to revel in his touch.

"How can I repay you? How can I help you? Like you helped me."

His words broke through the excitement I felt inside of me. I took a step back, shaking my head, and brushing imaginary dust off my dress.

"No one can help me."

"I was cursed by a witch more than two decades ago, and you saved me," he said.

I took another step back, eying him suspiciously. Nothing good ever came from a curse, and I didn't know what the after-effects of breaking one could be. I didn't need more trouble than I was already in.

"Why were you cursed? How did I break it?"

He shook his head, an almost melancholic smile on his face. "I was young and stupid. I insulted a witch, thinking I was invincible and nothing could harm me. Only the kiss of a maiden princess could break it, and you..." His eyes widened with realization. "You are a princess, you... What happened to you?"

I shrugged, turning away, hugging myself. "I wish it was something stupid as an insult," I sighed. "I refused to marry an evil wizard."

A tremble went through me, remembering those horrible first months of trying to survive, trying to find a way to break it. Since then I had resigned from my fate, and focused on my life, one day at a time. I had found joy in the little things, like watching the leaves as the seasons changed, gazing at the sunset and sunrise each day, and flying in my Swan form. There wasn't any better feeling in the world than flying over the forest, feeling the wind underneath my wings, and looking at the world behind it. Dreaming of a day I could rejoin the human world again.

The gentle hand of the man took me out of my musing. He turned me around and pulled me into a comforting embrace. I hadn't realized I had been shivering until his warmth surrounded me.

"When there is a curse, there always is a way to break it. Please let me know how I can help you."

His voice rumbled through me, as his touch soothed me. I tried to remember the day of the curse, what the wizard had said, but it had been so long ago. I shook my head and tried to step back, but he wouldn't let me.

"I don't remember."

He caressed my hair in a soothing rhythm, and I relaxed in his embrace. "That's okay. Let's try to see what you can remember. What's your name?"

"Odette," I said. I looked up and saw nothing but warmth and honesty in his beautiful brown eyes. He truly wanted to help me. "And yours?"

"Henry."

My eyes widened as a distant memory resurfaced. "You're the crown prince Henry that disappeared when I was younger."

He cocked his head, a sad smile crossing his face. "I guess I am."

"You were next in line for the throne." Another memory popped up. "You can help me," I said with a smile.

"That's amazing! Tell me how," he said excitedly, pulling me closer.

I suddenly became very aware of his very naked body against my thin dress. My nipples hardened, and brushed against his naked chest, as I could feel his cock rise between us. Clearing my throat, I pulled back slightly.

"I'm sorry," Henry said as he stepped back as well. "I didn't mean to..." he covered his cock with his hands, and smiled sheepishly at me. "I haven't been touched in a while, and I was a teenager when... Doesn't matter. How can I help."

I could feel my cheeks heat up, as I tried to tear my gaze from his hands, and what he was hiding behind them. I hadn't been touched in ages as well, and I missed his comforting warmth already.

"Don't worry," I said. "I get it. So you can help me, by uhm." I coughed suddenly aware of what I was going to ask. I took a steadying breath and looked him in the eyes. "By marrying me."

"Oh," Henry said nodding slowly. "I can do that. Is that all that needs to be done to break the curse?"

"Well, not all. I need to wed, and bed a king," I said remembering the words the wizard had spoken to me. "So when you become king, you could... maybe." I shook my head. "I'm sorry, forget about it, I am asking too much from you."

Henry stepped closer, pulling me into his embrace again. I sighed in delight, realizing how touch-starved I had been during the past years. His arms tightened around me, as I hugged him back. Caressing his naked back, my cold hands warmed up for the first time in forever.

"You're not, Odette. Without you, I would have hopped around for many years to come. Maybe you don't realize, but there aren't a lot of maiden princesses in the forest willing to kiss a frog."

I snorted, "Nor are there kings, willing to marry a swan."

His laugh rumbled through me, making me feel safe and cherished. We stood in each other embrace for a while, taking comfort from one another. We both ignored his erection and just focused on the pleasure of each other nearness.

When the sun rose, I had to let him go. Henry pulled my face slowly to him, giving me every opportunity to refuse. His lips touched mine, in a gentle, loving kiss. It was my first kiss if you didn't count the one in his frog form. A feeling of rightness filled me as his lips moved over mine. I moved with him, deepening the kiss, wishing it could last forever. Too soon I had to step back. When the sunlight touched me, I transformed back into my swan form.

Henry gently patted my head, in the same way I had done when he was a frog.

"I promise I will be back in a month, and we will break this curse together. Don't lose hope yet, Odette, I will help you."

With a nod from me, he left me behind alone again in the pond that had been my home for a decade. I didn't dare hope that he would be back, but he kept his promise. Less than a month later, when I was flying over the trees I could see the shimmer of armor, and a royal procession coming my way.

Henry arrived just before dusk, and as I flew down to greet him, I transformed and leaped in his arms.

"I wasn't sure," I said before I kissed him.

His armor felt hard, and unforgiving against my body, but his lips greeted me with the same softness and warmth as he had given me before. Our kiss soon turned more heated, as I poured all my passion, and desperation into it. I hadn't dared to hope, but now that he was here, I could finally open up my heart and let him in. Henry responded with equal passion, as his mouth opened, and his tongue joined the kiss. I moaned as I could feel his tongue seek out mine, and pleasure filled me. I would have let him have me right here and now if it hadn't been for the priest that cleared his throat.

We broke apart and smiled sheepishly at the man that could officiate our wedding. A few words, and formalities later we were husband and wife.

When we retired in the tent that his servants had prepared, my head almost spun.

"I can't believe this just happened, that we are now married."

"Do you have any regrets?" Henry asked as he removed his armor.

"What! No, of course not. Do you? I mean you could have any woman in the land."

When he was naked, he pulled me into his embrace, and I sighed when the comforting feel of his skin touched me.

"I have zero regrets," Henry said as he raised my chin so we looked into each other's eyes. "We were meant for each other. You have saved me, and I have saved you, and I hope we will continue to save each other with the trials yet to come." A haunted look crossed his face, as his brows furrowed. "I don't think anyone else could ever understand what we went through. But we will have each other."

"Yes, from this day forward, we are husband and wife," I said repeating the words the priest had spoken.

I caressed his forehead, trying to erase the worry from his face. Henry leaned in my touch and smiled. "Time to consummate our marriage, my sweet wife," he said.

A nervous shiver passed through my body, as I was not sure what he expected from me. I remembered vaguely the duties of a wife, but having never had to perform them I was scared to make a mistake. He noticed my distress and cupped my cheek gently.

"No rush, we have all night to figure this out," Henry said, easing my worries.

He was as inexperienced as me, and I could see the same nervousness in the twitch of his right eye. I nodded. "Thank you."

As we stood in silence, locked in an embrace neither of us wanted to break, I could feel my nerves calm. I looked around the gorgeous tent Henry had brought. The fabric was lined with gold, and the bed in the middle was filled with soft-looking pillows. My gaze drifted higher to the roof that had a hole in it, so I could still see the night sky.

"I had them make the hole when I realized I couldn't sleep without seeing the sky," he said, his cheek against mine as we looked up.

I understood, after spending a decade outside, it felt almost foreign to be in a room again. I was happy to be able to see the sky, and still hear the sounds of the forest. It was mixed with the sounds of his entourage, but the occasional buzz of an insect or squeak of an animal calmed me.

His hands started a slow dance across my back, soothing and rhythmic. I pushed the fabric of my dress off my shoulders, letting it fall to the floor. His breathing stopped for a moment when my naked body pressed against his, but then he resumed his caresses.

I grew bolder and started my own exploration of his body. His back felt smooth and warm underneath my hands, as I traced every muscle, and touched every inch of him.

His hands slid lower, cupping my butt cheeks, and making me gasp. His fingers tightened, as I took a small step to give him easier access. I could feel excitement rush through me, and my body responding to his touches. My nipples tightened, a warm feeling spread from deep within me and nestled above my pussy, as I felt wetness gather between my legs.

When I cupped his ass as well, he pulled me up to his body. My legs opened wide on instinct, and I wrapped them around him, rubbing my pussy on his hardening cock. We both moaned at the contact.

A sudden urge to have him inside of me burst through me. "Please," I begged.

Henry understood what I needed, and took two steps to the bed. As he gently laid me down, he positioned his cock at my entrance. He looked at me for reassurance but I nodded immediately.

"Take me, please," I said, as I pushed my hips up so he slipped inside of me.

His massive cock stretched me in the most delicious way, but my excitement and wetness eased the way. He groaned and pushed in deeper, filling me, and stretching me with all of him.

"Fast first, and slow later," Henry said and I moaned in response.

He pulled back, and thrust deep inside of me, making pleasure spark. Almost animalistic sounds left me, as he took my virginity, and made me his wife. Our bodies moved in a beautiful dance of lust and passion, as we became one.

Each thrust made me fly higher than I had before. Pleasure filled my every sense, and all I could feel and experience was my husband inside of me. Henry made feral sounds as he fucked me hard as I needed to be taken. I needed this to be fast, hard, and raw. This would break the curse, this would give me freedom, and tie me to Henry forever. Our fates would be mingled, and our lives shared.

It felt like we were made for each other in the ways that our pleasure grew, and crested at the same time. We both exclaimed our climax, and I could feel him fill me with his seed, as my muscles squeezed him tight. His cock pulsed, and his body shuddered, as I milked him with my pussy and shivers of pleasure washed over me. With a last thrust, he groaned and collapsed on top of me, embracing me, and covering me with his body.

I caressed his back, as the last tremble racked my body, and the pleasure faded away into a pleasant warmth.

"Give me a second, and I'll make sure that I'll pleasure you as a husband should," Henry mumbled in the sheets.

A laugh escaped me that caused me to tighten my muscles again. We both groaned as it made another spark of pleasure shoot through me.

"I think you already did, my dear husband. I can't imagine this getting any better."

Henry lifted his head and smiled. "But I have heard many stories and received many tips from my soldiers on how to pleasure a woman. And I intend to use every single one of these methods."

My cheeks heated up, as I imagined all kinds of scenarios on how he could give me pleasure. As I opened my mouth, and my stomach rumbled, he laughed and rolled off me.

"First food. Another way to keep my wife satisfied," Henry said.

"Food?" I asked, unable to imagine anything better.

He pulled a trolley from somewhere behind the bed, that was loaded with all of the food I had been dreaming of since I had been cursed. There were duck legs covered in sauce, fresh bread, red strawberries, and so much more.

We both feasted, feeding each other occasionally. As I was satisfied, I lay on the pile of pillows, basking in the afterglow of the food, and my orgasm. Henry started kissing down my body.

"Time for my dessert," he murmured as he kissed my breast. Circling the nipple with his tongue.

"What?" I asked, my voice breathless with excitement.

"I want to feast on my wife. I want to taste your pussy. I want to give you pleasure until you can't think anymore."

"Yes, please," I moaned.

Henry gently sucked on my nipple, until a spark of pleasure shot through me and I sighed.

"Cherries for topping," he murmured as he switched breasts.

My nipples were standing hard, rosy red. He pinched one nipple, as he laved the other with his tongue. I moaned, unable to stay quiet as he gave me pleasure in ways I hadn't imagined before. It seemed my husband's imagination was wider than mine, as he kissed his way down my stomach until he reached my pussy.

Henry inhaled my scent and growled. "I could just breath you in all night."

My body stiffened at his words. What if all we had was this night? What if we hadn't broken the curse due to some technicality? I would only know for certain when the sun rose that it had worked.

Henry felt me clench and distracted me in the best way possible. He licked me between my pussy lips, making me groan, and my back arch of the bed. It felt too good, I wanted to get away, but he held my legs firmly open so he could devour me with his mouth.

"Please," I begged, not sure what I was asking for.

"I'm here," Henry murmured against my pussy. "I am not leaving."

Somehow he knew just what to say to comfort me. I tried to banish the worrying thoughts out of my mind, and only focus on the pleasure he was giving me.

"I could stay here forever," he groaned as he licked me from back to front.

He opened my lips with his fingers and gently circled my pleasure bud with the tip of his tongue. A shiver of delight coursed through me, as he touched me in all the right places.

"Another cherry for tasting," Henry said.

He licked around the little bud until I was a moaning mess. When I felt like I couldn't take it anymore, he put his mouth on it and sucked. A very unladylike shriek came out of me, as my climax burst forth. Waves of pleasure washed over me, while he kept sucking on my bud. My whole body vibrated, and my muscles clenched around nothing. When the height of my orgasm flew away, I pulled on his shoulders.

"I need you inside of me," I begged.

Immediately he crawled over me, positioned his cock at my entrance, and entered me in one thrust. Another orgasm unexpectedly washed over me, as he filled me. My muscles squeezed around him, and he groaned. His body trembled with his control, but I didn't want him to hold back.

"Come, please, take me," I said.

My words unleashed something inside of him. He pulled back and started fucking me with an intensity that pushed me to another climax.

"Yes, yes, yes," I moaned, as he took me like a husband should take his wife.

"My wife," Henry groaned. "So beautiful, so tight, so ready for my cock."

I screamed in agreement as the pleasure took me away. I could only hear and feel him, everything else ceased to exist. He came with a guttural groan, and filled me with his seed, connecting us even more. He tried to pull off me, but I wouldn't let him go. I was terrified that as soon as I would release him, this all would turn out to be a dream. I needed his comforting weight and warmth on top of me.

Henry never went far from me throughout the night, and we made love several more times. I couldn't sleep, didn't dare to let him go. He understood without me having to speak my fears out loud. As the night passed, and dawn appeared, I asked him to take me again.

He entered me gently, making love to me as if we had all the time in the world. I closed my eyes, not daring to look. I didn't realize tears were appearing until he wiped them from my cheek with a gentle sweep of his fingers.

"I've got you," Henry murmured as he slowly entered me, and gave me pleasure.

My fingers dug into his shoulders, holding on to him, as the pleasure filled me. The orgasm was sweet and gentle, a little burst of pleasure that disappeared in the sea of desire we had created throughout the night.

"Look," Henry said after he had released inside of me. "Open your eyes, Odette. It's okay."

After a deep and steadying breath, I opened one eye and saw the sunshine fill our tent. I opened the other and looked down. The sun grazed my breasts, reflecting the light on my pale skin that hadn't touched sunlight in over a decade.

The curse was truly broken.

THE END

The Genie

What if Aladdin didn't find the Magic Lamp but Princess Jasmine did?

I HAD FOUND THE LAMP Jafar was looking after. It looked quite normal, but since Jafar wanted it I knew I had to get it before him. I turned it over in my hands, trying to figure out what was so special about this old oil lamp. It felt warm under my touch as if it had been laying in the sun all day. A spot of dirt caught my eye, and I took a piece of my skirt to dust it off. When I rubbed it, a rumble sounded from deep within. The lamp pulsed in my hands like a heartbeat, and with a startled gasp, I let it go. Instead of falling to the ground, it floated before me, and thick blue smoke came from the tip.

"Who has summoned me?" a deep voice vibrated through me.

A massive blue figure came out of the blue smoke and fixed its gaze on me. Piercing black eyes lay in a beautiful blue face. His hair, and beard were black, but his entire body until it disappeared into the smoke was blue like a clear sky.

"A princess. What do you desire? You have three wishes," he said as he crossed his arms and surveyed me.

He was shirtless, and by crossing his arms, his muscles bulged, drawing my eyes to it. His eyes roved over my body, making me feel seen for the first time in my life. A spark of desire burst through me, that I ignored. Three wishes could change everything. I could finally help my people. When I opened my mouth to answer he continued his monologue.

"I can give you all the riches you want," he said with a singing voice. He held open a hand and gold appeared in his palm. Coins, jewels, and diamonds glittered around him, lighting up the entire room.

"Or beautiful garments that everyone will be jealous of." He waved his other hand and rows of clothes appeared in every possible color and fabric. They floated towards me, trying to seduce me with their grandeur. As a princess, I already had everything I could dream of in materials possession. I didn't need more stuff that I would never use.

"Maybe a man to hang on your arm?" With another flick of his hand, a handsome young man appeared. "Hi, I"m Ala..."

"Stop," I yelled when it all became too overwhelming.

He quirked an eyebrow up and let his imaginary disappear. "Tell me what you desire, and I'll give it to you. You get three wishes that I will grant. I just can't make someone love you or bring anyone back from the death."

I nodded. I could use three wishes to help my people and get rid of Jafar. "How long do I have?"

He shrugged. "As long as the lamp is in your possession you get your wishes."

Knowing that Jafar was looking for it as well, I knew that I had to make my wishes soon. I didn't want to waste time or lose the lamp before I got to help my people.

I nodded, thinking about what I should wish for. "I want to help my people. How far do your powers reach?"

"Anything you can imagine, I can make true. You just have to rub the lamp, and say I wish," he said nodding to the lamp that floated before me.

I grabbed it and held it up to study it. It looked newer now, shining brightly as it lay warm, and heavy in my hand, pulsating as if it was alive. "How did you fit into this? You're so..."

"Magnificent?" he asked as he showed off his muscles while arching an eyebrow.

I laughed. "Big to fit into this tiny lamp."

"It is a tight fit," he said stretching out, enhancing his impressive muscles. I tried not to look at his magnificent form. I needed to focus on the wishes. "Comes with the job description. But magic makes it work."

"Magic, of course, I know that," I said with a smile. I already had the first wish ready. "Okay, if I can wish for anything in the whole world I wish to make my land fertile again so our harvests become plentiful."

He pointed. "Rub the lamp, and consider it done."

I rubbed the lamp and repeated my wish. A zing passed through me as I could feel the magic transfer from the lamp through me, and to the Genie.

He closed his eyes, crossed his arms, and nodded. When he opened them again I could see the black of his eyes shimmer with magic.

"It is done. Tomorrow the seeds will take root, and your next harvest will be successful. I noticed some dark magic tainting the lands so I got rid of that as well. Your crops should yield greatly for at least the next several generations."

"Thank you," I said and suddenly felt like I could breathe again.

My people would have food, and the promise of many more. I already knew what my next wish would be.

"Two more to go," he said holding up two fingers.

I nodded as I rubbed the lamp again. "I wish for the trading routes to open up again, so our economy can thrive."

The magic zinged through me, and his beautiful eyes lit up. "It is done. The next caravan will arrive in a month eager to rekindle the relationships between the nations."

Work that otherwise would take months, if not years just happened in the blink of an eye. There was only one thing left that I needed. When I wanted to make my last wish, the doors suddenly burst open, and Jafar and my father stormed in.

"What is the meaning of all this," Jafar bellowed, his screeching voice cascading through the room.

He saw the lamp in my hands, the Genie behind me, and I could see him connect the dots. He held up his serpent staff, but before he could say try to influence me with his magic, I turned to the Genie and rubbed the lamp. I had only a moment to decide but when I looked into his beautiful, piercing, but kind eyes I knew this was the only way. I needed to get rid of Jafar, and make my country prosper again. To be able to rule on the throne I needed a husband.

"For my third wish, I wish to marry you," I said while looking at my Genie.

"What?" sounded three voices.

My father sputtered, "But he is blue."

Jafar yelled, "Impossible."

The Genie just looked at me with surprise in his eyes when I could feel the magic zing through me, through him, and back through me. The smoke of his lower body disconnected from the lamp and turned into muscular legs. One of the golden cuffs he was wearing disappeared, and appeared on my wrist, locking in place with a click. The lamp in my hands shrunk and turned into a necklace that hung around my neck. I turned around to face my father and Jafar, feeling powerful.

"Now that I have a husband, I can become the ruler of this kingdom. My first action as ruler is to cast you out of my country Jafar. Leave and never come back, or there will be consequences."

Jafar ran to me, screaming in anger his robes dancing around him like wings of a bat. Before he could reach me the Genie suddenly stood before him.

"You will not threaten my wife. You will not touch my wife. You will not even look at my wife!" he bellowed, and in the next moment Jafar disappeared in a puff of blue smoke.

"Where did he go?" my father asked, as he looked around him. "What happened?" as he looked at the Genie, now my husband, with glassy eyes. Jafar's magic had influenced him for many years. "Who are you again?"

"You can call me Jinn," the Genie said as he extended his hand. "And I appear to be your son-in-law."

"Oh, right, right. Welcome. I think I'm going to lie down for a while. My head hurts. You'll be great a great Sultana dear," he said looking at me. "You're mother would be proud."

"Thank you, Father. You go rest. I'll make sure to make you proud."

When my father left the room I was suddenly alone with my husband, Jinn.

"So do you accept my proposal?" I asked. "I don't want to force you into anything by using my wish for it."

Jinn stalked towards me as my tiger did to his prey. I shivered but stayed put. I would not cower before any man, my own husband including. Standing before me, I had to arch my neck to be able to look him in the eyes. Even standing on the ground, not floating anymore, he looked absolutely massive. Up close I could see that his blue skin looked velvety soft, and I couldn't wait to roam my hands over his body. I've never wanted a man more in my life than him.

My Genie lifted up his hand, putting a finger underneath my chin to tilt my head even higher. A gasp escaped me when his skin made contact with mine, and I could feel the magic, and something more vibrate through me. Desire filled me, as my body swayed closer to his. His smell was intoxicatingly spicy, and I could feel my body react to him. My nipples puckered, my pussy clenched, and I could feel wetness gather in my panties. I had to do everything in my power not to moan out loud.

Jinn studied me with a piercing gaze and seemed to like what he found. He bowed lower until our lips almost touched, and I could already taste his spicy breath.

"I accept," Jinn said, and in the next moment his mouth touched mine.

The moan that had been building up inside of me burst out when his touch, smell, and taste encompassed me. Our bodies melted against each other as our mouths devoured one another. He was like a man on the brink of starvation and my mouth was the one thing to feed him. Our lips touched, our teeth clashed, and our tongues danced around. It was like a beautiful dance of two souls coming together.

My hands crept up his arms towards his massive shoulders, while his encompassed my waist, and held me close to him. His body felt incredibly hot against mine, but if I were to get burned this would be the best way.

Arousal rose inside of me as I could feel his cock harden against my abdomen. I gasped for breath when our mouths disconnected. My heart was beating a thousand miles a minute while my whole body vibrated with the need for him.

"Don't humans have customs on their wedding nights?" Jinn asked me.

He waved his hand and suddenly my room was decorated with all kinds of beautiful flowers. A mirror appeared in front of my bed, framed by burning floating candles. Baskets of decorated food stood beside my bed, music sounded from somewhere in the night, and I could smell the faint smell of rose water, and burning incense lingering in the air. It was all perfect, but too much for me.

"All I need is you," I said as I lay my hand on his cheek, stroking it with my thumb. "I need someone to be by my side while I rule this country, and doesn't try to overpower me. You will have all the freedom you can dream of, all the riches you can use, and you'll have me."

Jinn pulled his arms around me and lifted me up. "All I need is you, my wife. You have given me freedom. You have released me from my shackles, and have given me mortality again. I am bound to you and will be for all of your life. This is more than I could have ever dreamed of, and it is all thanks to you. It might have been out of a necessary evil that you made that last wish, but that one wish made all mine come true."

"Let's consummate our marriage, so no one can ever tear us apart," I said, and I kissed him again.

This kiss was sweeter, slower. Jinn savored my lips as if he wanted to memorize my taste. His tongue met mine, and his delicious taste exploded in my mouth. I moaned as his spicy taste, and smell filled my senses.

"My wife," Jinn mumbled against my lips as his hands roved over my body.

Every kiss and every touch sparked pleasure inside of me. I never wanted this to end. All I experienced was him, all I could think about was him, and all I could taste was him. My hands discovered his body as well. His skin felt velvety soft underneath my touch. A low rumble sounded from his chest as I let my hands glide over him.

"My husband," I said.

"I need to taste you," Jinn said.

With another flick of his hand, I was suddenly laying on my bed. The breath wooshed out of me as he appeared before me in the air. His eyes roved over my body, taking in every inch of me.

"So beautiful, and all mine," Jinn whispered to himself.

I didn't know how he still had his Genie magic, but I didn't care as long as he used it like this. The next moment my clothes were gone, and my husband was between my legs. I moaned when I could feel his tongue part my pussy lips, and taste my juices. Pleasure sparked inside of me when he touched me in places I had never been touched before.

"Yes, all yours, please my husband," I moaned.

I didn't know what I was begging for, I just knew that I didn't want him to stop. He growled against my pussy, making vibrations pass through me, and pleasure spark deep inside of me. His tongue was like a magic wand, experienced to find every pleasure point in existence, and triggering it. Every swipe, lick, and flick of his tongue made more pleasure rise.

It felt like a damn that was ready to burst, but I wasn't ready to let go yet. I didn't want this to stop. I've never been pleasured, and having this magnificent man, on his knees between my legs, did things to me I couldn't explain. I wanted to scream, moan, beg, and do all kinds of things I had never done before. It was as if he knew that I was holding back because he lifted up his head, abandoning my pussy, and looked at me with his piercing black eyes.

"It's okay to let go, my sweet wife. I'll be here to catch you."

Before I could reply he dove back down and pleasured my pussy with his talented tongue. Pleasure shot through me as he circled my clit with the tip of his tongue, while he thrust a finger inside of me. His words had been just the thing I needed to be able to let go, and when the next wave of pleasure crested I let myself be washed away with it.

With a pleasured cry the orgasm shook my body, making me tremble, and squeeze my pussy around his thrusting finger inside of me. I could feel more wetness gush out, but Jinn licked it up with hungry groans. Pleasure filled my every sense, and for the first time in my life, I let someone else take control. I experienced it on a cloud of freedom as wave after wave of pleasure washed over me.

Jinn made sure that my body could relax as he wrung out the last of my climax with his mouth. Little aftershocks of pleasure racked my body as he gently caressed me, and enveloped me in his arms. I sighed happily as I let myself relax against his strong, warm body.

"That was amazing," I mumbled against his chest as I placed gentle kisses on the small piece of skin I had access to.

"You are amazing, my sweet wife."

I looked up at the serious tone of his words. His thoughts seemed to be miles away as he stared into the distance. I touched his cheek, directing his gaze towards me, trying to eradicate the ghosts of his past with a gentle caress.

"How long were you in that lamp?" I asked.

He angled his head, pressing my hand closer to his skin. "A thousand years," he said. "But I was glad to be in the lamp as opposed to dealing out the wishes of my previous masters. Each and every single one of them always wanted power and riches. Nothing was ever enough. But you," Jinn said and caressed my cheek. "Your first two wishes weren't even for yourself."

I shook my head. "You're giving me far too much praise. It is my duty as princess, and now as sultana to look after my people."

"You're giving yourself too little praise my princess, my sultana, my wife. Far too many people would have chosen themselves over anyone else, but you didn't. I am honored to be able to call myself your husband. If I could choose between an eternity alone or a lifetime with you, I would always choose you."

"Oh Jinn," I breathed, never having received such a heartfelt compliment in my life. "I'm so happy I found your lamp."

"Me too," Jinn said and he kissed me.

Words were lost after that as we discovered each other bodies in the quiet of our wedding night. Our tongues danced, as our kiss grew more heated. My hands roved over his body, loving the feel of his soft skin underneath my fingers. His hands encompassed my breasts, scorching my nipples, and hardening them in the process.

"I want all of you," I moaned as I reached for his loose pants.

I could feel his rock-hard cock ready to burst underneath the soft fabric, and couldn't wait to see it. Would it be blue, and massive like the rest of him? My hands got lost in the multitude of fabric, and I huffed out an annoyed breath.

"Can this come off?" I asked as I pulled at the offensive fabric.

"Your wish is my command, my sweet wife," Jinn said.

With a flick of his wrist, he was naked, and I could admire him in all his grandeur. His cock was as magnificent as the rest of him. It was big, blue, hard, and stood up straight, ready to give me pleasure. I wanted to taste him before he would focus on my pleasure again. I pushed him on his back and crawled down over his body until I reached his impressive length.

"What do you want?" Jinn asked and with another swish, his cock grew. "Bigger? Smaller? Longer? Harder?"

With every word, his cock changed shape, from normal to impressive to laughable. I grabbed it in both my hands, cutting off his next proposal.

"Just as you were," I said.

Jinn groaned and changed it back to its original state. I smiled as he trembled underneath my touch. An all-powerful being was like putty in my hands when they were on his cock. His cock felt heavy and hard in my hands, and I couldn't wait to feel it inside of me.

I leaned over to lick the tip, earning a strangled moan from him. His delicious taste exploded in my mouth, even more, potent than our kiss had been. He tasted like my favorite herbal mixed with my favorite spices. A unique and delicious blend specifically catered for me.

"I have survived the fall, and rise of kingdoms, and dynasties, but your mouth will be my undoing," Jinn groaned as he buried his hands in my hair.

I giggled, and licked him again, moaning as more of his taste filled my senses. I caressed the rest of his length with both my hands while I licked his tip with pleasure. With steady movements I caressed his cock, loving the sounds that came from him with every caress.

His cock throbbed underneath my touch. I let my hands wander lower, reaching his balls, heavy with his unspent seed. I cupped them, massaging them gently as I put my mouth over his tip, and sucked.

With an earth-trembling roar, my Genie came and filled my mouth with his seed. I moaned as I sucked, and sucked to get every drop of his delicious seed. I felt powerful, to be able to make him come this quickly with just my mouth and hands.

Jinn pulled me up when I had squeezed the last of his seed from his cock. His mouth met mine in a passionate kiss that took my breath away. He didn't seem to mind his own taste mixed with mine.

"My wonderful, amazing, wife," Jinn murmured against my lips.

In one move he turned us around and positioned his cock at my entrance.

"Yes, take me, make me yours," I moaned as I put my legs around his hips, and grabbed his shoulders.

In one thrust he filled me with his amazing cock. I moaned as my pussy stretched to accommodate his massive girth. It felt like he went on forever, filling me inch after delicious inch. Pleasure and pain were mixed inside of me, but pleasure prevailed when he pulled back, and thrust back inside of me, giving me even more of him.

"So tight," Jinn groaned.

Jinn touched every pleasure point inside of me with his cock. Each thrust made me relax more and gave him the ability to fill me up more until he was finally in the hilt. It felt like his cock was made to be inside of my pussy, fitting perfectly just at the edge of comfort.

"Yes," I moaned. "Give me all of you."

He groaned low, as he fucked me harder. With a moan, I squeezed my pussy around him experimentally. Never before had I felt so full, but it felt too good to describe. Jinn growled as my pussy milked his cock, thrusting into me harder, and faster. Every drag of his cock, sparked pleasure inside of me. My room was filled with the sounds of our bodies coming together, and our exclamations of pleasure.

His black eyes burned bright with passion, as he fucked me, and we consummated our marriage. Pleasure rose inside of me with a speed that made my head spin. It would be only a matter of moments before I would come again. I could feel my pussy pulse around him, trying to draw him in deeper each time he pulled out.

"I'm going to come," I moaned as I could feel the pleasure wash over me.

"Yes, my beautiful wife, come on my cock," Jinn growled and fucked me with even more determination as if he wanted to leave an imprint of his cock in my pussy.

A strangled cry left me as pleasure washed over me, filling my senses. My body trembled, and my back arched off the bed as my pussy squeezed him hard. I could feel his cock throb inside of me, and after a few more thrusts he came as well, filling me up with his seed. My pussy milked him, giving us both even more pleasure with this joining.

The sound of our pleasure cascaded through the room, making sure that everyone knew that we had consummated our marriage. Jinn was mine, and I was his, forever from this day forward.

THE END

Peter & Pan

What if Peter & Pan grew up and revisited Wendy?

A LOUD THUD WOKE ME from my sleep. It was the middle of the night, and I lay in my bed, listening to see if I heard it again. A soft knock on my window urged me to get up. I grasped the soft linen of my curtains, and with one move pulled them aside. Through the glass of my terrace door, I could faintly see the outline of a familiar figure. Without hesitation, I opened the door, and he lost his balance. I could barely stop him from hitting the ground. His weight took me down, but I caught him in my arms. Instantly I knew who he was, I would have recognized those green eyes everywhere.

"Peter," I said.

"Wendy," he sighed, and his eyes fluttered close.

With some effort, I was able to direct him to my bed. When his head hit the soft pillow, he moaned softly.

"Please, Wendy, help me."

"What happened?" I asked.

I kneeled on the floor beside my bed, holding his hand as I studied his face. Almost a decade had passed since I had last seen my first love, but it looked as if he hadn't aged as much as I had. He seemed to be just on the brink of adulthood while I was firmly planted in it.

"They all left me. Hook took Tink, and then you left and everything went wrong. The magic started fading. I lost everyone, and I started growing old." He opened his eyes, a haunted look crossing his face. "Look at me," he whispered. "I'm not a child anymore."

I swiped away a whisk of his blond hair from his forehead, and with a soft smile, I nodded. "Neither am I. But there is so much to experience in life."

He shook his head and closed his eyes again. "I will not hear it. I didn't use the last of my pixie dust to be lectured by you, Wendy."

I sighed, dropping my hand on the sheets. He hadn't changed a bit. Everything had to be his way. He was always right, and everyone else was always wrong.

"Then why did you come, Peter?"

"I need your help to find my shadow."

I rolled my eyes. Of course, it was because he needed my help. Not because he missed me, or that he realized he felt the same feelings I did when I left.

"How did you lose him this time?"

"I don't know. I woke up one day, and it was gone. I only realized I had started growing older when I went to the mermaids, and they didn't recognize me anymore." He gripped my hand and held it against his cheek. "Please, Wendy. You are the only one that can help me. I have no one left."

I stroked his face with my thumb, feeling the rough texture of a stubble graze his cheek. He wasn't a boy anymore.

"I will help you. Now rest."

With my reassurance, he fell into a fitful sleep. I got up and went outside on my little terrace overlooking London. With a sigh, I pulled my dressing gown around me. This wasn't how I had imagined our rekindling to be.

I remembered our farewell. We had laid together in the field of daisies, our fingers intertwined, gripping each other as if we would never let go. When I closed my eyes, I could almost smell the soft floral scent mixed with the magic of Neverland. The scent of darkness disturbed my memory. A shiver washed over me, and the hairs on my neck stood straight. Without opening my eyes, I knew who was standing behind me.

"Hello, Darling," his guttural voice filled my ears.

I bit my lip to stop screaming. My heartbeat sped up, and I could feel my muscles tense in the fight-or-flight reaction. Just as I made my move, he grabbed me. His hard fingers dug into the skin of my hips as he lifted me, pushing me against the railing of my terrace. My feet weren't touching the ground, and the unwavering metal dug into the soft flesh of my belly.

Arousal coursed through me at the all-too-familiar feeling of his powerful hands holding me steady. My fingers gripped the metal of the railing in an attempt to maintain some illusion of control, but he was in complete control. He chose if he held me or tipped me over to the street below.

My heart raced in my throat as I opened my eyes, and saw how far down the ground was. One lone car rode through the night, illuminating the street, but when it turned the corner, it was dark. It was a cloudy night and only a solitary streetlight flickered in the night, giving London an eerie glow.

"Don't scream, or I might let you fall, Darling."

My pussy clenched at his rough voice, and I barely contained the moan that was building up inside of me.

"Who... who... are you," I said, trying but failing to keep my voice steady.

He tsked in my ear. "So you remember Peter, but not Pan?"

Of course, I remembered Peter's shadow. We spend many nights together talking, laughing, and doing so much more. He was as similar to Peter as he was opposite. They both had that mischievous streak that earned them the title of King of Neverland. Everyone hung on their lips with every word they spoke. When Peter said right, Pan said left, but somehow I had fallen for both of them.

His hand slid lower over my hip to between my legs. A soft moan escaped me as he cupped my pussy, and I could feel wetness gathering in my panties.

"Remember now?" he whispered as he let his tongue glide over the shell of my ear.

A shiver coursed through me as his fingers lifted the thin fabric of my nightgown. A growl escaped him when he found me wet and ready for him.

"Please," I moaned, not sure what I was begging for, but he knew. He always knew exactly what I needed.

"Please what? Say it, Darling."

"Please, don't stop," I said.

"Never, my Darling."

He circled my clit with his finger, creating pleasurable tremors all over my body. Pan knew how to play my body like his favorite instrument.

"Are you so wet for me or for Peter?"

I moaned in response, not even sure what the answer was to his question. He and Peter were undoubtedly linked, and I had feelings for them both, but it was hard to distinguish them. His finger dipped lower into my aching entrance. My pussy clenched around his finger as if trying to suck him inside. Pleasure rose inside of me with his every move.

"Such a needy girl," he said, and added another finger.

I bit my lip to keep myself from begging for more, but he already knew what I wanted. He pushed a third finger into my pussy, stretching me, and filling me. His thumb strummed my clit, and my climax came closer and closer. I could feel the pleasure ball up deep inside of me, rising with every touch of his talented hand. My breasts ached, and I could feel my nipples poke through the soft fabric of my nightgown. The cold London air cooled my heated skin, and the hard, unwavering metal underneath my hands and belly kept me present in the moment.

"Are you going to come for me, Darling? Are you going to come all over my hand out in the open? If one of your neighbors looked out of their window right now, would they see you come by the hands of a shadow?" he asked, increasing the movements of his hands.

His thumb pressed harder on my clit, as he curled his fingers inside of me, touching my pleasure points inside and out. His low growled words were my undoing, and I could feel my orgasm take over.

"Pan, please," I moaned as pleasure burst inside of me.

Waves of pleasure washed over me as he kept strumming my clit and fucking me with his fingers. My toes curled, and my knuckles turned white with the strength I was holding onto the railing. I bit my lip to keep from screaming out my pleasure to all of London. My body trembled as my pussy clenched around his fingers inside of me.

"Yes, come for me Darling," he growled as he fucked me harder, wringing the last of my orgasm out of me.

A last shiver of pleasure washed over me, and he slowly pulled out his fingers. My pussy clenched around him, trying to keep them inside of me. I moaned when I felt empty without him stuffing me.

"That was..."

"Magical," he said and put me down.

He turned me around, holding me steady when my legs threatened to buckle underneath me. His black form surrounded me, and his glowing eyes sucked me in.

"Pan," I said.

"Darling," he said in a soft tone that I hadn't heard before.

I saw something cross over his face, but it was gone before I could identify it. He held his hand in front of him, and sucked off his fingers one by one, making decadent sounds in the process. My pussy clenched as I saw him devour my juices, wishing he would go straight for the source.

"Delicious," he said.

Before I could reply, he turned around and walked into my room.

"Let's wake up this fucker, and get sowing."

With a sigh, I followed him. I needed some time to process what had just happened, but Pan didn't give me any. He kicked Peter, who mumbled groggily and presented me with a golden needle.

"Made out of Pixie dust," Pan said. "Only thing that will ensure that it sticks this time. As much as I despise him, I do need him."

I accepted the needle and started sowing. The repetitive motions calmed me and gave me time to gain my composure. I couldn't let them walk all over me again. But what did I want? I needed to protect my heart because I didn't think I could survive losing them both all over again.

When one foot was attached, I looked up to see both men studying me with steady eyes. Peter had some more color on his face now that he was reunited with Pan. He studied me with heat in his eyes that made my pussy clench. Pan was always harder to read, but there was something in his eyes that made me feel warm from the inside. I could feel my cheeks heat up, and I looked down again, focusing on the second part of the sowing.

As soon as I made the last stitch, Peter and Pan jumped up and flew around my room. They grabbed me on the second turn and hugged me close. The last Pixie dust fluttered around us and made me go up in the air.

"Thank you so much, Wendy," Peter said as he made a summersault with me in his arms, making the butterflies in my stomach rise.

A reluctant laugh escaped me at his enthusiasm. I felt safe in the embrace of both of my men. It almost felt the same as when we were young.

"Let's show our girl our gratitude in a more pleasurable way," Pan said behind me.

"Your girl?" I asked as excitement fluttered through me.

Pan hugged me from behind, pushing his growing erection against my ass, and mushing me close to Peter, who wasn't as unaffected as he tried to play.

"Of course. You don't think I am letting you go, now that I have found you again?" Pan asked.

"But what about me?" Peter asked, looking at me, and Pan behind me.

"What if I want you both?" I asked, gazing into Peter's eyes and grabbing Pan's hand.

"Us both?" Peter asked.

"I think we need to make it up to our girl for making her wait so long for us to grow up. There is nothing left in Neverland for us, and we have everything we need here with her," Pan said, his voice surprisingly soft.

I looked behind me, seeing the warmth in his glowing eyes. "You'll both stay?"

"If you'll still have us," Pan said as he caressed my cheek.

A smile broke through my face, and I could feel the butterflies in my stomach. "Yes, of course," I said and kissed Pan.

The kiss soon turned heated as he grounded his erection against my ass, and I moaned in his mouth. Pan tasted of black licorice and sandalwood. Another hand gently cupped my cheek. I broke the kiss, and let Peter direct my mouth to his. I moaned into the kiss as his apple crisp taste filled my senses. Two men so very different, but absolutely perfect for me, and all mine.

The tearing sound of fabric filled my room, and suddenly my nightgown was gone. The pieces of fabric floated to the ground as I was still levitating above the floor. Four hands roved over my naked body as Peter plundered my mouth. One pair of hands massaged my breasts as the other pair slid lower. One hand cupped my pussy while another probed my other hole. I gasped and broke off the kiss when a finger entered me where I had never been touched before.

"Will you let us claim all of you, Darling?" Pan whispered in my ear while one of his fingers slowly thrust into my ass.

It was a strange, and new experience to have something up there, but not one I was opposed to. Peter's mouth descended over my neck, to my collarbone, and discovered my breasts. I was a moaning mess, being pleasured by two men at the same time.

"Yes, please. I'm all yours," I managed to say.

"You're so beautiful," Peter murmured while he looked at my breasts with a reverent gaze.

He cupped them in his hands, caressing the hardened nipples with his thumbs. My breasts ached, and pleasure sparked with his ministrations of them. I flew higher in the air as more pleasure filled my senses. Pan slid down over my back, kissing every inch of me he discovered. Soon he came to my ass, kissing me, and licking me in my most intimate place. I had to put one hand up so I wouldn't bump into the ceiling, as my other grabbed Peter's hair to have something to hold on to as both men rocked my world.

Peter's mouth, lips, and tongue played over my breasts as if he was mapping out the best trajectory for my pleasure. Pan was using his hands to pull apart my ass cheeks and dive into his new treat. His tongue did magical things to my back door, and I could feel the pleasure rise deep inside of me. Sounds left my mouth that I didn't even recognize. My pussy was a sopping mess, and it wasn't even touched by either of them. I had never imagined being able to orgasm without my pussy being played with, but my men were on the fast track to prove me wrong.

"So delicious," Pan said.

"Absolutely exquisite," Peter said.

I just moaned in response. They didn't want an answer anyway. They were too focused on pleasuring me and making me a moaning mess of desire. I loved everything they did, and could only experience what they were giving me. The ball of pleasure inside of me was getting bigger, and bigger with every move they made.

"Are you going to come for us, Darling?" Pan said before he pushed his tongue in my ass, making me delirious with pleasure.

"Yes, please," I moaned as pleasure sparked inside of me.

"Yes, Darling. I want to feel you come around my tongue, and then I want to feel you come around my cock," he groaned and started fucking me with his tongue.

Peter was so lost in his focus on my breast that he didn't even take part in the conversation. His tongue circled my hardened nipple as his fingers tweaked the other, sparking pleasure deep inside of me. I gripped his hair tighter, as I could feel the climax rise.

My whole body felt like it was on fire. I was experiencing too much at the same time. The soft caresses of Peter on my breasts, and the insistent fucking of Pan's tongue in my ass was too much for me.

Within moments, my climax washed over me, and I cried out in pleasure. My whole body trembled as my pussy and ass clenched tight. Pan murmured, content as he could feel my orgasm. He licked me slower, drawing out my pleasure, and giving me a moment to breathe. Peter kept pleasuring my breasts with the same urgency until I gently pushed his head away.

"Give me a moment," I sighed.

Pan pushed him harder when he didn't listen to me. Pan grabbed Peter's face and pulled it up.

"Kiss her, and then fuck her," he growled.

Peter immediately obeyed his shadow, and his mouth devoured me with the same passion as he had kissed my breasts. I moaned into the kiss, accepting his tongue inside of my mouth.

Pan's hands roved over my quivering body, soothing my muscles and calming me down. He came up behind me, pushing his rock-hard erection against my ass.

"We're going to fuck you so good that you don't even know where you begin, and we end," he whispered in my ear.

A shiver of desire washed over me at that whispered promise. Peter plundered my mouth, as I could feel Pan slip his cock between my legs. His dark hands grabbed my hips, angling me backward so he could dip his cock inside my pussy. I moaned into Peter's mouth while Pan's cock stretched me wide to be able to take him.

"Such a tight pussy," he growled. "I'm going to love fucking your ass."

He slid in deeper, giving me every inch of him, sparking pleasure inside of me. I wanted all of it. Everything they did to my body was pure pleasure, and I wanted everything they could give me. My pussy fluttered around his cock as he kept filling me with more of him. It felt like he went on forever, fitting inside of me perfectly.

"So wet," Pan groaned when he bottomed out inside of me, stuffing me full with his amazing cock.

He gave me two amazing thrusts, sparking pleasuring inside of me before he pulled out. I moaned into Peter's mouth at the loss, but I was immediately rewarded with the feeling of him probing my ass. His cock was slippery with my juices, but it was still a tighter fit.

I grasped Peter's shoulder, kissing him, and trying to relax while Pan slowly slid inside my ass. He gave me inch after delicious inch of his cock. It burned in the best way, giving me pleasure like I've never experienced before. But I wanted more. I wanted them both.

I broke the kiss and panted. "Fuck me, Peter."

He didn't need to be told twice, and immediately grabbed one of my legs, pulling it around his hip, and positioning his cock at my sopping wet entrance. My pussy stretched to accommodate his girth while already being filled by Pan. In one move, Peter entered me, and I was stuffed by both of my men.

They both groaned when I tightened around them, and I loved the sounds of their pleasure. I've never felt so full, and so complete before. It was almost as if my body was made to fit these two men perfectly. My body trembled as pleasure filled my senses.

"Fuck you feel amazing, Darling," Pan said.

Nonsensical sounds came out of me, as Peter and Pan growled when my pussy and ass clenched around their cocks.

"Wendy, you're beautiful," Peter moaned.

I could only imagine what I must look like, suspended in the air fucked by Peter, and Pan, surrounded by man and shadow. When they started to move it felt like a short circuit went through my brain. I could only feel and experience pleasure as they moved in tandem. One pulled out, and the other entered me, creating the most delicious friction deep inside of me.

"Tease her clit," Pan growled. "Make our girl come around our cocks."

Peter immediately obeyed, pushing his hand between our bodies and circling my clit with his talented finger. My pussy clenched around his cock as pleasure sparked inside of me.

"Wendy, you're squeezing me so hard," Peter moaned as his movements became more urgent.

Pan followed his rhythm, and both cocks pummeled into my body, hard. Pleasure sparked deep inside of me, and I knew it would only be moments before I would come again.

"Come for us, Darling," Pan growled in my ear as he fucked my ass faster.

His rough words were enough to send me flying over the edge. I moaned as my orgasm washed over me. My body trembled, and my pussy and ass squeezed around my men's cock, earning me strangled groans and curses. Waves of pleasure washed over me as they kept fucking me, and Peter's fingers strummed my clit like it was an instrument. Everything felt overly sensitive, but incredibly pleasurable at the same time. I didn't even know who was saying or moaning what. All I could experience was pleasure.

A few thrusts later, my men came as well, filling me with their cum. Their cocks throbbed deep inside of me, while their groans sounded like music in my ears.

We floated to the bed, sated with pleasure. The cold sheets cooled my heated skin, while two pair of arms surrounded me in the best hug I had ever had. Still stuffed by their cocks, I fell asleep between my two men, Peter and Pan.

THE END

The Fae Guardian

What if Cinderella didn't have a Fairy Godmother, but a Fae Guardian?

I RAN INTO THE NIGHT with the tattered remains of my dress clinging to my body, and the shrill laughs of my step family behind me. How could anyone be so cruel? All I wanted was to go to the royal ball, just for one night. I wanted to dance and look at all the pretty dresses. Creating memories I could cherish forever while working under the bitter rule of my stepmother. But they wouldn't even let me have that. They ruined my mother's dress, insulted me, and chased me out of the house.

My throat hurt as a sob threatened to break through. I ran blindly into the forest adjacent to my family's home. The familiar scent of nature calmed me, while it felt like the moonlight warmed me. Without realizing where I had gone, I had come to the weathered stone bench I used to sit on with my mother. I let myself fall down on the cold, but soft forest floor, and lay my head on the bench.

The tears that I had held back while my stepfamily hurled cruel words at my head, flowed freely, covering my face, and hands in salty wetness. I would allow myself this one moment of sorrow, and then I would pick myself up again, and continue like I always did.

"There, there, sweet girl," a soft, melodic voice spoke in the night.

I didn't bother to turn around. I needed to compose myself before I could face whoever was there.

"Please, leave me alone," I begged.

"My apologies, my sweet girl, but I was hoping you could lend an old man a hand."

I turned around and saw an old frail man, hunched underneath a tree, his leg stuck behind a branch.

"Oh, I'm so sorry," I said, jumping up and wiping my tears away.

My own sorrow was momentarily forgotten as I focused on the poor man in front of me. With some effort, I was able to free his leg, which had a nasty cut on it. I tore off a piece of my ruined dress to bandage the cut. When his leg was covered, I led him to the stone bench, supporting his surprisingly heavy weight.

When he sat down on the stone, he grabbed my hand with an uncharacteristically firm grip and pulled me beside him.

"Even in your darkest hour, you always put another first, Ella," he said, as he cupped my cheek with his warm hand.

The familiarity that he had in using my name startled me, but I remembered the way my parents had raised me.

"Of course. For where there is kindness, there is goodness and where there is goodness, there is magic."

"Your mother used to say that," the old man said with a smile.

"Who are you? How did you know my mother? How do you know my name?" I asked, pulling back from his tight grip, suddenly wary of this old man.

With a theatrical move of his free hand, his appearance started to change. With a gasp, I watched the magic flow around the forest like shooting stars, transforming him into a handsome man with sparkling blue skin, and white hair.

"What are you?" I asked in wonder.

"Which question do you want answered first?" he asked with a wink.

"Whichever you want to answer," I said.

He shook his head, taking my hand again. "Always putting the other person first. You remind me so much of your mother. I am your Fae Guardian. When you were born, your mother made me promise to always look out for you."

When he saw the scratch marks on my arms, he tsked. With another move of his hand, I could feel a warm glow spread around my arm, and in a moment the pain faded, and the marks were gone.

"Thank you," I said, touching the spot where my skin had healed.

"I have to apologize, Ella. If I had realized how badly they treated you, I would have done something sooner. Your spirit always seemed to be so high. Whatever they threw at you, it never dulled the light in your eyes. Until tonight," he said, brushing a strand of hair from my cheek.

I could feel a blush rising with the way his gorgeous blue eyes looked at me. Never before had a man stared at me so intently before. Not looking at the dirt on my face or the state of my clothes, but really looking at who I was on the inside. Seeing Ella, and not Cinderella as my stepfamily had dubbed me.

"No need to apologize," I said, breaking his gaze.

"But I do, Ella." His soft touch underneath my chin forced me to look into his eyes again.

The guilt in them made my heart ache, but there was something else, something darker that I couldn't, wouldn't identify. His gaze made my body come alive for the first time in forever. Before I could do something stupid, like kiss a stranger, I forgave him with a word and asked about my mother.

"Your mother was one of us, a Fae. She left the forest when she fell in love with a human. Something I never understood before, but seeing you now, I can."

"You're too kind, dear sir," I said, trying to break my gaze, but his eyes sucked me in.

"Please call me Varden. I am in no aspect a gentleman," he said, his voice a darker undertone to it than before. A shiver passed through me, but I wasn't scared of him.

"A pleasure to meet you, Varden."

"Believe me, my dear Ella, the pleasure is all mine," he said and pressed a soft kiss on the top of my hand.

A warm tingle spread from the place he kissed through my body and nestled low in my stomach. It felt unlike anything I had felt before. I quickly pulled my hand back before I asked him for another kiss.

"So what does a Fae Guardian do, besides stalk me, and see me at my lowest point?" I asked, gesturing at my ruined dress.

"Ah, that is the fun part," Varden said and jumped up. With another twirl with his hand, I could feel the magic sizzling in the air. "I can make all of your dreams come true."

I opened my mouth to say that I wouldn't even know what to wish for, when lights twirled around me, caressing my skin. I could feel the fabric on my body change and transform. In mere moments, the shredded fabric had become the most magical dress.

I stood up, twirling around to see the full extent of his mastery. I was wearing a gorgeous gown that still had elements of my mother's dress, but he somehow transformed it into the most regal-looking garment I had ever seen. It had the color of the night sky, a fitting bodice that hugged my every curve, and a flowy skirt that seemed to go on for miles.

"Varden, this is... I have no words."

"No need for words, my dear Ella. I know that all you wanted for this evening was to dance and create memories that would last you a lifetime. Let me give you that tonight."

With another whirl his woodland clothes were exchanged for a royal outfit, fit for a prince. He extended his hand and bowed to me.

"May I have this dance?" Varden asked.

I accepted his hand and was pulled into his embrace. His nearness took my breath away, and when I looked into his eyes, it felt like I could fall into them forever. The forest sounds around us became melodic, carrying a tune that I recognized as one of the folk dances that were custom on a ball. I didn't know the steps, but with Varden's firm hand in mine, and on my lower back, he guided me through it.

We danced through the night, laughing together, until I could hear the faint sounds of the town clock striking midnight.

"Oh, I must go, before my stepmother returns," I said, pulling back from his embrace, but his firm hands wouldn't let me go.

"No, Ella, please. What is it that you truly dream of?" Varden asked, our lips a hairbreadth apart. "I know you want more in this life than to be the servant of people who don't deserve your kindness."

My heart was going a thousand miles a minute, and I was sure he could hear it beat in my chest. I hadn't dared to dream of something beyond my current life, afraid that the heartbreak would be too much to bear after losing my parents. But in the safe embrace of his arms, I finally dared to dream of a life bigger than this. A life where I could be free, where the house belonged to me as it should rightfully be, and I could help people other than my stepfamily.

With a gentle smile, he cupped my cheek. "It will be so." Varden waved his arm again, and I could feel the magic in the air. "Your stepmother is going to meet an Earl at the ball, and by tomorrow they will be gone, leaving the house to you."

"How did you know?" I asked.

"Because a dream is a wish your heart makes, my dear Ella. And for the first time in forever, you dared to dream of something for yourself."

Suddenly I felt lighter, knowing that the burden of my step-family was gone. "There is something else I want," I said, daring to dream of something more.

"Anything, Ella. Anything at all."

"I want you," I said and slowly pushed up on my tiptoes, closing the distance between our lips.

Varden tasted like the forest, and my dreams mixed in a delicious cocktail. His lips were soft but firm underneath mine, and after only a moment of hesitation, he took control of the kiss. He pulled me up in his arms, deepening the kiss. I opened my mouth in a gasp, and he immediately took advantage of it by plunging his tongue into my mouth. I moaned when our tongues met, and passion sparked.

This was my first kiss, so I had no possibility of comparing, but I just knew that this kiss was the start of something new, and amazing. Now that I was finally free, I would grab life with both hands and enjoy it how I wanted it, with Varden.

He broke off the kiss, panting, holding my body flush against his. I could feel something hard digging in my stomach, and arousal coursed through me, imagining what would be underneath those layers of fabric.

"Are you sure, Ella? I don't want you making a mistake with me," Varden said.

"More sure than I have ever been of anything in my whole life," I said and kissed him again.

He made a wholly sensual sound against my lips, a low rumble of pleasure that I could feel tremble through my body. I could feel more magic flow through the air, but I didn't want to break our kiss to look. Moments later, we were lying on a soft surface, his warm body covering mine. His lips followed a path over my chin to my neck, licking and kissing every spot he encountered.

I opened my eyes and saw that we were lying on a majestic four-poster bed in the middle of the forest clearing. It looked like it was made out of branches that had woven itself together to create a gorgeous artwork. Flowers sprung from every corner, tinting the air with their sweet floral scent. The mattress we lay on was created from moss and was incredibly soft to the touch.

I wanted to marvel at the beauty Varden had created, but his mouth distracted me. His lips had reached the edge of my dress, and with a small tug, my breasts popped out from their confinement. A guttural moan escaped me when his lips closed around one of my nipples. His tongue laved the soft bud in gentle licks, making pleasure rise inside of me.

"You are delicious," Varden growled against my naked skin.

A faint throbbing started in my pussy with each flick of his tongue, and I could feel wetness gathering in between my legs. My other breast ached for the same attention, while all I could do was moan in pleasure. As if he understood my wordless plea, he switched breasts and licked my other nipple. Another pleasurable sound escaped me while he licked and kissed my breasts. His hands and mouth worked together to ensure that both my breasts were pleasured equally.

Never before had I felt such pleasure. My insides felt like they were ready to burst into a million pieces, but I was scared of my own desire. I didn't know what to say, how to react, or what to feel, but Varden guided me through it.

"Just let go, my sweet Ella," Varden mumbled against my skin.

I obeyed his command, and let myself fall of the edge. My muscles relaxed, and suddenly the pleasure inside of me burst. I felt a soft glow of pleasure fill me, but not like the explosion that I had read about in books. It felt amazing, better than I had ever experienced, but it wasn't groundbreaking or life-altering.

"Just feel," Varden said, and kissed me, breaking off any thought that would distract me from the pleasure.

His lips grounded me, making me let the pleasure flow through me with every breath.

"That was..." I didn't even know which words to use to describe the sensations.

"Only the beginning, my dear. There is so much more to discover together if you'll have me."

"I want all of you," I said and pulled him down for another kiss.

I was already addicted to his mouth and the comforting feel of his big body on top of mine. I wanted to feel more of him, all of him, but our clothes were in the way. With an annoyed huff, I tried to expose his skin, but the buttons didn't want to work with me. Varden noticed my struggle, and with another wave of his hand, we were suddenly naked. I could feel his warm, and soft skin against mine, and I moaned at the contact.

My hands immediately went in search of the hardness that I had felt before. When my fingers closed around his rock-hard cock, a pained groan erupted from his throat.

"By the Gods, Ella. Your hands feel like magic," Varden groaned, as he broke our kiss and pushed his forehead against mine.

His warm, and heavy breaths fanned over my face, as my hands discovered his straining erection. He felt unbelievably big, and I was almost afraid to look at him. His cock throbbed in my hands, and I could only imagine the pleasure of feeling him inside of me.

"I want you inside of me," I whispered against his lips.

His eyes sparked with passion as a hungry groan came from him. "I want that too, Ella. More than anything, but I need to make sure you are ready first."

His body slid over mine, and I had to let go of my newly discovered prize. I made a soft sound of disappointment, that soon turned into one of pleasure when his mouth connected to my pussy. He pressed a soft kiss on my mound before gently opening my lips with his fingers. I was already so wet from my first orgasm that he easily slid between my lips. Varden groaned when his tongue connected to my sopping pussy.

"Already so wet for me," he said between licks.

"Yes, please, Varden," I moaned, opening my legs wider.

For never having experienced the pleasure a man could give me before, I was eager for more. His tongue did heavenly things between my legs, sparking pleasure with each flick. The build-up inside of me was bigger than before. I wasn't sure what would happen, but I trusted him with my whole heart.

After having licked my whole pussy, and the surrounding area, Varden suddenly focused on my clit. A startled gasp escaped me as the pleasure rose faster inside of me. My clit throbbed, begging for his attention as if it was the focal point of my pleasure. Sounds I've never made before erupted from my throat as my body trembled with his ministrations.

My sounds seemed to spur him on as he focused more intently on my pleasure spot. With another flick of his tongue, the damn inside me suddenly burst, and pleasure washed over me. This time, it felt like how it was described in every story I had ever read. My muscles relaxed, and the pleasure inside of me burst into a thousand pieces, filling my every sense. Trembling all over, I felt waves of pleasure wash over me. My breath stopped for a moment as my brain tried to comprehend what had happened.

Varden kept licking me, coaxing more and more pleasure out of me, until I moaned in surrender. He gently let me come down from my high, caressing me, and kissing me softly all over my body. His mouth reached mine, and another soft kiss grounded me. I could taste my essence on his lips, mixed with his delicious taste. I kissed him again, wanting more of him.

"I want you inside of me," I said, craving more of that pleasure, but together with him.

I had already experienced so much amazing feelings that I wanted him to join me in it. I needed to feel his gorgeous cock fill me up like no man had ever done before.

A pained look crossed his face when I grabbed him. His hand covered mine, and he made one sad attempt to pull me off. The next moment, his hand guided me in the best way to pleasure him with firm strokes.

"This is not a good idea," Varden groaned with his forehead against mine, breathing heavily.

"Why not?" I asked.

"We Fae bond for life, and I do not think that is what you want right now."

I stared back at him in defiance. "My whole life, people have told me what I want, and what I needed. Dictating my every move. Now I choose for myself, and I choose you."

"You are too kind to me," Varden said as he caressed my cheek. "You know nothing about me."

"I know that you're the first person to see me as a woman. To speak to me as an equal. To treat me with a kindness that I have always treated others with. Is that not enough?" I said, gripping him tighter.

His breath came out in pants, and his face looked tortured, but his eyes sparked with pleasure.

"I do not know, my sweet, kind, Ella. Only you can decide if I am enough for you."

"I do," I said and kissed him while stroking his cock.

His hand covering mine pulled me off before I could give him the pleasure that I wanted.

"If you want me inside of you, you should stop now before I burst into your hands."

"Yes, I want you inside of me, and then I want you in my mouth," I said.

He groaned, kissing me with so much passion it took my breath away. "You absolutely gorgeous woman. You are too good for me."

Varden gently eased me down on the bed again, spreading my legs so he could kneel in between them. For the first time, I had a good look at his equipment, and I had to swallow when I saw how big it was. I had felt it in my hands, but towering over me like he was now, it seemed even bigger.

As if reading my mind, Varden said, "We'll go slow, my love. You are already nice and wet, and ready for me."

He leaned over me, positioning his cock at my entrance. With slow movements, he stroked my pussy with his cock, coating him in my wetness and giving me a moment to get used to his size. There was nothing I wanted more in this moment than him inside of me.

"Please, Varden. I need you," I moaned, opening my legs even wider.

He growled low, and before I could beg again, he pushed the head of his cock against my entrance. It felt frighteningly massive, but with a hard push, it entered me. I could feel myself stretch to accommodate his girth, and pleasure spark with the intrusion.

"It's so big," I moaned.

"That is only the tip, my love," he growled and pushed further, giving me more of him.

Pleasure and pain mixed while Varden stretched me more and more with each inch he gave me. Sounds of desire and passion came from me without them making any sense. I wanted more, needed all of him, and he understood me. So very slowly, he fed me inch after inch of his delicious cock. My pussy ached and stretched, but somehow he fit inside of me. When his final inch filled me, I couldn't breathe, being so stuffed full of his Fae cock.

Varden gave me a moment to get used to his size while gently kissing away the pain. I suspected he used some of his magic to ease my ache, but I had no words left to say, being too consumed by pleasure. When he pulled back and thrust back inside of me, pleasure rushed over me. My pussy clenched around him, as if trying to keep him inside. Varden groaned and seemed to lose his composure, suddenly fucking me harder.

I moaned and begged, and loved every single thrust he gave me. My body was pushed into the soft moss on the bed, while his big body covered mine. He growled low with each thrust, sparking pleasure inside of me. His beautiful face contorted with passion, and his eyes burned bright with desire.

Another climax was fast approaching, but I needed him to join me in it. I squeezed my pussy around him with each thrust that bottomed out inside of me. His strangled groans of pleasure showed that my plan was working. The urgency behind his thrusts increased, and he fucked me harder and faster. Suddenly it became too much for me, and a white-hot climax ripped through me. My body trembled, my back arched, and my toes curled with pleasure as my pussy quivered around him.

With an earth trembling roar, Varden came with me. I could feel his cock throb deep in my pussy, bathing my insides with his release. More pleasure filled me as his climax mixed with mine. Our bodies were locked together at the height of our passion, never wanting to let go of each other.

The force of the orgasm shook me to my core, and more pleasure than I could have ever imagined filled my ever sense, as Varden was buried deep inside of me. When the last tremors shook his body, and my pussy milked the last of his release from him, he let out a deep contented sigh.

With the last of his strength, he rolled us over, me on top of his chest, still connected to each other. I sighed with satisfaction as I laid my head on his chest, listening to the quick beat of his heart.

"I am never letting you go now, Ella. You are mine," Varden vowed.

"There is no place that I would rather be than with you, Varden," I said, closing my eyes, basking in the afterglow of the most amazing climax of my life.

I was happy for the first time and had hope for the future. My future with my Fae Guardian, my Varden.

THE END

The Dragon

What if Rapunzel was guarded by a Dragon who fell in love with her, and helped her get out of her tower?

I WOKE UP TO THE HEAVY breaths of my dragon riffling my curtains, and his comforting smoky scent filling my tower. With a smile, I jumped out of bed and started my morning chores while signing.

"Good morning, Tanwen."

"Good morning," he replied, his voice clear as day in my head.

I was lucky to have my dragon, otherwise, the days in my tower would be very dull. "What is on your schedule today?" I asked while sweeping the floor like I did every day.

I passed the only window in the tower that was filled with one of his big red eyes. Sometimes it was hard to grasp how massive he was. I usually only saw a small part of his face or his tail when he swooped away on one of his excursions.

"Nothing special," Tanwen replied. "What will you paint today?"

"Oh, I don't know yet. Maybe inspiration will strike when I am done with my chores. I prepped the south wall yesterday, so I have a blank canvas ready for my brush."

"Do you need more paint supplies or a specific color?" Tanwen asked, like he did every day.

I checked my supply, noticing a bright red that had been tucked away behind the others, and inspiration struck. I looked at my window and back at the wall. They were almost the same size, and the red was almost an exact match with Tanwen's color. I could already visualize the brush strokes needed to create his eyes on the wall.

"No, I have everything I need, but I do want to ask for a favor today."

A low rumble sounded from deep within his chest as he shifted on the tower, and I could feel the stones vibrate underneath my feet.

"Anything for you," he said.

"I want you to be my model for the day."

His big eye blinked slowly, and he remained quiet for such a long time that I thought he hadn't heard me. When I opened my mouth to ask again, he answered in a serious tone.

"It would be my honor. What would I need to do?"

"Absolutely nothing," I said, already gathering my paint supplies, brushing away my hair. "You just have to stay right where you are. Unless you had an excursion planned today?" I asked, looking back at his gigantic eye.

"As long as you have food and paint, I do not need to leave today," Tanwen said.

"Okay, perfect."

I immediately started with the outline of his massive eye on the wall. While I was painting, Tanwen told me tales of his past. He had been cursed to be a dragon by a witch many years ago, condemned to guard this tower. I loved listening to him while I painted. My dragon had been with me my whole life and he was the only one that I knew besides the witch who visited once a year.

In a few weeks, she would come again to cut my golden locks. If my birth parents hadn't been as desperate as they had been, I wouldn't even be here, but I also might have never existed. My mother had been ill with a very rare disease that only the golden eggs of a magic goose could heal. My father had stolen them from the garden of the witch, and as punishment, they had to give me up. Now I was living in this tower, a possession of the witch much the same as that golden goose had been. Each year my hair grew longer, and the moment she cut it off with her magical scissors it turned to gold.

I had long since resigned to my fate. The only lights in my life were my paintings and the company of Tanwen. Focusing on his eye, I noticed how beautiful it was. Every facet of red shone in his eyes, reflected by the sun. I'd seen it a thousand times before, but now his eye seemed different somehow. As if just staring into it could suck me into his stories, free from this tower. I immediately stopped the thought before it could get away from me. It was dangerous to dream of something I could never have.

"Do you ever dream of flying away and not coming back?" I asked while I had my back turned to him, pushing away my hair so I could reach the wall.

"Never," his voice sounded angry in my head.

"Why not?" I asked, not looking at him, hoping he wouldn't see the emotions that clouded my voice.

"I could never leave you, Rapunzel. You would-" It was almost as if he couldn't even say the word out loud.

We both knew that without his steady supply of food, I would perish away. "Thank you", I said, my voice a little quieter than before.

"If I had the power, I would whisk you away, and show you the world," Tanwen said with a fierceness in his voice that I hadn't expected.

I turned around with a smile, almost tripping over my hair. "I would love that. But we both know we shouldn't dream of things that will never be."

I went to the window, touching the spot of scales that I could reach. His warmth spread through me, and not for the first time I imagined how it would be if he could join me in the tower. He could curl around me, keeping me warm with his internal flame, and I would finally know how the touch of another would feel. I shook my head, banishing the thoughts far away, and went back to my painting.

A stupid knight who tried to save me only disturbed once us, but Tanwen made quick work of him. I was tired of princes and knights thinking they could just rescue me from this damned tower. As if I wouldn't have tried leaving it myself. The magic seal on the window the witch created prevented me from even going across the windowsill.

By the time it was dark, I could barely hold my brush anymore, but Tanwen's eye was finished. I still needed to do the window, and the space surrounding it, but I was happy with my progress. I had looked more at his eye in one day than I had ever done, and when I fell asleep, it followed me.

My dream differed from my usual one. I always dreamed of freedom, being outside of the tower, imagining how the world might look like, and if it would be like in my books. But this night I dreamed of my tower, my bed, and a mysterious red man that joined me between my sheets.

I couldn't see the figure's face, only one big red eye that was staring at me. The familiar feel of Tanwen's gaze on me made me feel relaxed, and safe to let go. My dream soon turned erotic. Phantom hands I couldn't see were touching my body in places I hadn't explored before. I could feel arousal rise inside of me, and I was excited to see where this dream would lead me.

My nipples hardened with the soft touch caressing them. I could feel a moan bubble in my throat, but I was afraid that if I made any noise, the figure would disappear. The touches were soft like a whisper, but enough to arouse me like never before. They circled around my nipples, making them throb with pleasure, aching for a firmer touch. I could feel wetness gather between my legs and I hoped that the phantom touches would go lower over my body to the place where I ached the most.

As if it could read my thoughts, the caresses glided down over my breasts, to my stomach, and finally to between my legs. A soft gasp escaped me when it touched my pussy. I was so sensitive there that even the whisper of a caress was enough to spark pleasure.

I opened my legs wider, giving more access to my dream lover, and he immediately took advantage of it. A firmer touch between my pussy lips made me jump, startling the figure that disappeared immediately.

I woke up with a moan, disappointed that it had ended too soon. Tanwen's eye was staring at me as usual, but the blush creeping up my cheeks was new. I was still flustered by my erotic dream, and I wasn't ready to face reality yet. My heart was racing, and I knew I was wet between my legs. I wished I had a moment alone to relieve my ache, but Tanwen's steady gaze was on me. Before I could ask him to leave, he spoke first.

"Did you mean it yesterday? When you said that, you would want to see the world with me."

The question threw me off since my mind was still reeling from my dream, but I answered truthfully.

"Yes, with my whole heart."

Would he notice that my voice was huskier than normal or that my heart was beating so fast? He blinked slowly, and after a moment of staring at me, he nodded.

"Very well. I will be away for some time. Will you be okay alone?"

"Yes, you don't have to worry about me," I said, waving his worries away.

"I am going to need a small piece of your hair."

"Take as much as you need," I said, pulling my sheets up higher.

His tail entered the tower, grabbing a piece of my hair. The moment he cut off a strand with his talon, it turned into solid gold. He had used some of it before to pay for some supplies for me, so I didn't think much of it.

Without another word, he flew away, leaving me alone in my tower, still in my bed. I didn't want to dwell on his strange behavior, because I needed to find my release first. I pushed my hands between my legs, finding my pussy wet and aching. A moan escaped me when I swept my index finger over it in an exploring motion. I had never done this before, but the actions of the figure in my dream were still etched in my mind, so I mimicked those movements.

I slowly spread my pussy lips with my hand, exposing it to the cool air in the tower. With my other hand, I explored my folds, searching for that pleasurable feeling from my dream. Everything was sensitive and felt amazing with my finger caressing it, but I discovered a little bump that was more sensitive and felt better than anything else. I focused on that spot, circling it with my finger, gently discovering what felt good and what felt amazing.

Pleasure rose inside of me with every movement of my finger, and soon I was panting and moaning, aching to reach my release. My pussy was contracting around nothing, as my clit felt swollen and more sensitive to each touch. I needed to fill that aching feeling inside of me and used one of my fingers to search for my entrance. A gasp escaped me when I entered my pussy for the first time, more pleasure filling my senses. I wanted more. I needed to be filled with something more. Adding another finger ached for some of my need, and stroking my little bump only enhanced the feeling. My hips were rising of their own accord, and my hands and fingers were moving faster and faster. I could feel the pleasure inside of me build, and build, ready to burst.

I opened my eyes and looked at the painting I had made the day before. With Tanwen's gorgeous eye gazing at me, making me feel safe and cherished, I could finally let go. With another flick of my finger over my pleasure bud, the pleasure flowed over me. I screamed out Tanwen's name as my whole body trembled, and my pussy squeezed around my fingers. Everything inside of me wanted it to be Tanwen, even though I knew it was impossible.

With a sigh that was filled with pleasure and loneliness, I let my hands fall on my bed. My body hummed with pleasure as my mind was filled with longing for something I couldn't have.

After my reinvigorating orgasm, I started on my usual chores. When I had finished those, I worked on my painting. I didn't need Tanwen since I had finished his eye already, but I would have enjoyed his company. My tower felt lonely without him. When he still hadn't returned to join me for dinner, I was starting to get worried. He had been gone for longer periods, but then I had known where he was. Now I wasn't sure. I fell into a restless sleep, void of Tanwen's eye or the mysterious figure.

The flapping of Tanwen's wings woke me up. I immediately jumped out of my bed, almost tripping over my hair, not caring that I was only wearing my thin nightgown. I ran to the window, jumping over my hair. It was only just dusk, so it was hard to make out his figure, but when he came closer, I saw that he was carrying a small package in his claws. I stepped aside so he could throw it through the window.

With a thunk, the package hit the floor, and my curiosity won it from my relief at seeing Tanwen again. I opened up the package when my dragon landed on the tower, and the comforting rumble of his claws against the stone calmed me.

"Where have you been?" I asked, while opening the package. With a gasp, I held up the most beautiful paintbrush I had ever laid eyes on. The stem was a dark red, like the shade of Tanwen wings, and the brush's hair was golden. "It is beautiful. What's the occasion?"

"Which question do you want answered first?" Tanwen asked, calm as always.

I huffed. "Both."

His low chuckle made the tower vibrate, and I smiled at his big eye covering the window.

"I was with a witch," Tanwen said. I gasped, but before I could express my concern, he continued. "She is a good witch. She cannot break our curses, but she has found a way that we could share them. The brush is made from one of my talons, and your hair. If you paint me in human form, I can transform."

I stared in amazement at the brush. Now that he mentioned it, I did recognize my hair. I touched it, surprised at how soft it was while transformed into its golden state. I never really paid much attention to it. As soon as the hair wasn't connected to me anymore, it didn't feel like my own. The stem was beautiful, and looking closer at it, I could see all kinds of sigils carved into it.

"Why would a witch help us?" I asked.

"Because she doesn't want the evil witch to win this battle. After I am transformed, I can join you in the tower so you are no longer alone, and..."

His hesitation caught my attention. "And what Tanwen? What aren't you telling me?"

"If you wish to be with me, I can turn you."

"Turn me? How? Into what?" I asked, excitement coursing through me. If there was even a small possibility of leaving this tower, I would grab it with both hands.

"The witch said that if we came together, and I bite you at the height of your pleasure, I can turn you into a dragon. That way, we share each other's curse. But only if you want, Rapunzel. I would never expect you to do something that you do not want."

I stepped towards the window, grabbing the brush in one hand, and touching the small part of him that I could reach with my other. It was hard to speak with so many emotions whirling around inside of me. All I had ever dreamed of was freedom, and to be able to experience that together with Tanwen was even more than I could have ever hoped for.

Tanwen took my silence as a refusal and started to pull back. "I am sorry. I should not..."

I silenced him with a kiss on his scales. "There is nothing in this world that would make me happier than spending the rest of my life with you away from this tower, in whatever form that would be."

"It would be my honor," he said.

I immediately started to work to create a fresh canvas on my walls. It needed to be big enough to capture all of him. I was contemplating how I would paint him.

"What do you want to look like?" I asked.

In a moment, he sent me a visual in my head of a man with red skin and the head of a dragon. I gasped when I realized it was the figure from my dream.

"It was you all along?"

"I needed to know how you would react to me. If you would be interested in me in that way."

The figure became clearer, and when I looked down, I couldn't contain my moan. Tanwen had two cocks that seemed impossibly large. I put my hands on my cheeks, feeling the blush creep up on them.

"I didn't know you could do that."

Now I wished my dream hadn't been cut short, and I would have experienced all of him.

"I have only ever visited you in your dreams when you had a nightmare."

I remember having a dragon watching over me in my dreams from when I was little. I just never imagined it had been Tanwen all along.

"You've protected me all my life, by day, and by night."

"I would do everything for you, Rapunzel."

"I don't know what to say."

"You do not have to say anything. Please, just paint so I can finally hold you in my arms."

I did just that, taking extra care when painting his cocks. I imagined how they would feel inside of me. I've only just discovered my own pleasure, and now I was already imagining more of it with him. Each cock had its own special texture that was hard to convey on the wall with my paint, but I tried my beast. The top one was thinner, but had ridges that would feel heavenly with each and every thrust. His lower cock was thicker and had scales covering it like his tail.

My hand trembled, outlining both, and wondering if he would use both on me. Tanwen had to bite me at the height of my pleasure, and being fucked by both cocks would be more pleasurable than I could even imagine.

Hours later, with hardly any break, I finished the lifelike painting of Tanwen in his transformed form. The moment I put down the brush, I could feel the magic swirling through the air. My hair lit up, filling the tower with a golden shine. Tanwen's roar made the ground rumble. Smoke and a burning scent filled the tower, and suddenly Tanwen stood before me just as I had painted him in all his naked glory.

I ran over, jumping in his arms, reveling in the feel of his scaly embrace surrounding me. He was warm and real, and being hugged by him was the best feeling in the world. He buried his snout in my hair, inhaling my scent, and almost crushing me in his hug.

"You are so soft," Tanwen murmured as his hands traveled over my hair, my back, and my arms, touching every part of me that he could.

His voice sounded smooth but had a smoky quality to it that I hadn't noticed when it was in my head. I loved hearing it out loud, filling my tower with sounds that were made by someone else.

I could feel something hard poking in my belly, and I chuckled. "You're not."

"I have dreamed of this moment for so long, and this new body knows it as well. I want all of you Rapunzel, body, mind, and soul."

I put my hand on his elongated mouth and smiled. "I'm all yours."

A low growl sounded from him, but instead of rumbling the tower, I could feel it rumble inside of me, sparking pleasure and desire in a way I hadn't experienced before.

"I am never letting you go," Tanwen said, tightening his grip on me.

"Please don't. I never want to be alone again."

His thin lips touched mine, and I was being kissed for the first time in my life. It was a bit strange kissing him since he had such a long snout, but we made it work in the best way. His tongue flitted out from his mouth, caressing my lips, coaxing them to open. I moaned into the kiss, accepting his tongue from my mouth. It had a strange but pleasurable texture and form so very unlike my own. Our tongues touched and danced around each other, licking, tasting, and experiencing each other for the first time.

His hands roved my body while our kiss turned heated. It was as if he was touching me everywhere at once, still not believing that I was really in his arms. His tail rested on my ass, supporting my weight so his hands could discover every part of me. I reveled in the feel of him all over my body. After not being touched for so long, every touch felt like a breath of fresh air.

With a few steps, he was at my bed, and he gently put me down on it. I didn't want to let him go, grabbing his arms to keep him from going too far.

"I am not leaving you, Rapunzel. I just want to get you naked," Tanwen said.

"Oh, okay. That's fine," I said, helping him remove my garments.

In a moment, I was naked, and his warm red eyes roved over my form. I was suddenly very aware of my body and I wanted to cover myself up, but before I was able, his hands touched my breasts. A gasp escaped me as pleasure rose with his touch. My nipples were sensitive and hardening under his scorching caress. His hands were textured due to the scales that covered them and created unique sensations with his touch.

"You are beautiful," Tanwen said, looking me straight in the eyes. "I have always thought and I always will think that you are beautiful in whatever form you are."

"I think you're beautiful, too. And strong, and brave, and kind," I said, cupping his cheek with my hand. "And all mine."

"All yours," Tanwen agreed, before focusing on my breasts again.

His clawed fingers gently pinched my nipples, making me gasp with pleasure. He growled low at my reaction, bowing his head to let out his tongue to play as well. His tongue was forked and textured, and unmeasurable long. It kept coming out of his mouth, circling my breast, almost covering it whole. The twin tips of it circled my nipple, lightly pinching it as he did with his hand on my other breast. It was such a similar, yet different, experience. I moaned with pleasure, not sure how he could make me feel like this. He let his tongue slide off me, licking my breast on its way.

"Delicious," Tanwen growled before going for the other.

My breasts were wet, but I wasn't cold due to his amazing body heat, warming me with the slightest touch. I wanted more of him, so I pulled him on top of me. His comforting weight covered me and made me feel safe and cherished.

"I want to lick and devour you for all of eternity," Tanwen groaned, licking my breasts and going lower down my body.

"Yes, please," I moaned. I wanted to be devoured by him, my dragon, but I also wanted to do some devouring myself. "I want to taste you too," I said.

A full-body shiver took over, and I could feel him rumble low. "I will not last if you put your hands on me, Rapunzel. Let me first see to your pleasure."

"But your pleasure is my pleasure, Tanwen," I said with a pout.

"And I will have mine soon enough. Please let me taste you first before I lose my control and fuck you like a monster."

I gasped at the rough words coming out of Tanwen's mouth. He was always so gentle with me, but I knew that he was hiding something darker away. I licked my lips, swallowing before I found my voice again. When I spoke, it had a husky tone to it that didn't sound like me.

"What if I want you to fuck me like a monster?"

His snout was close to my pussy now as he growled low. His warm breath fanned over my wet, throbbing pussy and it was as if it lit a fire inside of me. I opened my legs wide, showing him all of me. A blush crept up on my cheeks, but my gaze remained locked on him.

"I want you to fuck me, Tanwen," I said.

Those words were enough to break his resolve. His body covered mine as his hands pulled my legs wider apart so he could kneel in between them.

"I can never deny you anything, Rapunzel," Tanwen said before he placed his top cock at my entrance.

I was wet and aching for him and I didn't want to waste another second. I locked my feet behind his legs and pulled him closer to me. His hot cock made contact with my pussy and we both moaned loudly.

"Please, I need you inside of me," I panted.

He grabbed his cock, aiming it at my entrance, and very slowly inched inside. He was massive, too big, too much. It felt as if he was splitting me apart and a scream tore from my throat as he stretched my pussy to be able to take me. He immediately stopped, although his whole body was trembling with the last control he had.

"Don't stop. Please," I said, trying to pull him closer with my legs, but he wouldn't budge.

There was no way I could move this massive dragon with my strength, but my pleading words would. "It will only hurt for a moment, I know. Please give it to me. I need you."

With an earth trembling growl, he thrust forward and filled me in one move. My breath was pushed out of me as pleasure and pain filled me. Tanwen kissed my face, licked my breasts, and did everything he could to distract me from my pain, murmuring apologies over and over. After a moment, the pain faded and only pleasure remained. I moved my hips to signal him to fuck me, and he did. When he noticed that my discomfort was gone, he braced his hands on the bed, pulling back and thrusting in me.

Sounds of pleasure left me that I had never heard before, but it was all because of him. My dragon with his wonderful cock that was fucking me to an inch from my life. Pleasure sparked inside of me, filling my every sense and taking over any clear thought that I had.

His low grunts only enhanced my pleasure. Knowing that I was doing this to him and that it was my pussy he was fucking made me feel honored. I could feel the pleasure rise inside of me with each thrust of his cock. It all became too much for me. His delicious cock filled me so perfectly, the pleasured sounds he made, and the feel of his heated body moving over mine. With a startled cry, my orgasm took over, and pleasure surrounded me. My pussy clenched around his cock as my body trembled.

His cock throbbed, and Tanwen filled me with his seed. He pulled out and immediately placed his second cock at my entrance, pushing inside. Our mixed juices eased the way for his slightly larger cock, but I still moaned loudly when he stretched me. Pleasure filled all of my senses, and all I could feel was his cock carving space into my pussy.

He growled low as he pulled back and thrust inside of me again. Pleasure sparked with each move. My hands were clawing at his scales, needing something to hold on to as he rocked my world. My second orgasm was already fast approaching, and I could see that he was having trouble holding back as well. I didn't want him to hold back. I wanted all of him.

"Fuck me harder," I moaned.

Tanwen's eyes turned dark with lust and he fucked me faster. He pushed my body into the soft mattress as he covered me and drilled me with his second cock. Pleasure burst inside of me, and my climax washed over me. His cock throbbed, and he filled me with his seed to the point of overflowing. We were making a mess of my bed, but I didn't care. Soon I would be gone from here, joined with Tanwen, both dragons, and free from this tower that held me for all my life.

"I want them both," I moaned, the words escaping my lips with a mix of longing and certainty, as if my very soul understood the intricate connection between desire and the power of magic.

"Are you sure, Rapunzel?" Tanwen asked.

"Yes, please give me both. Fuck me, and mark me as yours," I said, sounding like a wanton woman.

Only a few hours ago, I had been a virgin condemned to live alone in my tower for all of eternity, and now I was ready to take both cocks that my dragon had to offer. I was ready to be marked by him and turned into a dragon.

He growled, grabbing both his cocks, slick with our combined juices, and positioned them at my entrance. I moaned when I could feel the hot heads graze my already abused pussy. He slowly pushed inside of me, stretching me, and sparking pleasure with both his cocks.

Sounds of pleasure and desire left me as my whole body quivered while he sunk his cocks inside my pussy. When he bottomed out, he held himself still, eyes on me, checking how I was doing.

"I'm going to mark you now, Rapunzel," he said, his whole body trembling with control.

He was holding back for me, checking in to be sure that I was ready for him. I've had both his cock inside of me, and now I was being double stuffed with them at the same time. A bite on my neck would hardly be the thing that would break me.

"Yes, please, turn me," I said as pleasure washed over me while he moved.

At the height of my pleasure, I could feel his teeth pierce my skin and fire fill my veins. I gasped as the magic swirled through me. My whole body trembled and tensed with the rush of pleasure, pain, and magic flowing through my body. I was connected to Tanwen in the most intimate way possible. My pussy squeezed around his cocks as he filled me with his seed and his magic.

He pulled out his cocks and teeth and gently laid me on the bed. I could feel my body transforming. Tanwen held my hand as everything inside of me burst. My hair wrapped around me, illuminating the tower with a golden shine. The soft strand of my hair caressed my skin and fused to it, changing me into something new, something strong. I became a massive golden dragon. With an earth trembling roar, I broke free from the tower that had held me as a prisoner for so long. In moments, Tanwen's red dragon form joined me.

"You are beautiful," his voice sounded in awe inside of my head.

I looked down and saw golden scales covering my body. Stretching, I noticed I had wings, a tail, and so many amazing new features. I was free, and I was stronger than ever.

"Let's go get that witch," I said.

He smiled, showing off his dangerous teeth, lifted his head and roared into the heavens. I could feel the air tremble around me, and I joined him in his call.

Despite our curses being joined, we were free, and together forever.

THE ENd

Authors Note

I can't believe I have already finished my second fairytale collection! I still have some ideas left so I do really see a third one in the future. The first one for my next collection is already in progress!

I can never pick a favorite, and I love every single one that I wrote!

Anyway, I hope you enjoyed the story! Please leave a rating and/or a review if you did!

About the author

Lilith Leana writes what she loves; Monster, fantasy, and sci-fi erotica. Born and raised in Belgium, she devours ebooks as if it heals her. In her day job she loves to organize, plan and make schedules for other people, but when the night falls she can let loose with her fantasies which star all kinds of Monsters and Human couplings.

YOU CAN ALSO FIND ME on:

New Author Website: https://lilithleana.wordpress.com/

New Newsletter! Sign Up to be kept up to date about my new releases, sales, character art, and giveaways: Sign Up Form[1]

Instagram: https://www.instagram.com/lilithleana/

Etsy Shop: https://www.etsy.com/be/shop/SteamyPublishing

Or you can email me: lilith.leana666@gmail.com

DEAR READER

If you enjoyed this book, please consider leaving a review. Indie writers depend on reviews to keep writing and publishing.

Thank you so much ♥

Lilith

Also by the author

Series & Collections

Fairytale Retelling Short Stories

---

1. https://books2read.com/u/47gLkj

2. https://books2read.com/u/47VMwA

3. https://books2read.com/u/bW0pk1

4. https://books2read.com/u/3LxQD1

5. https://books2read.com/u/4AA7Zp

6. https://books2read.com/u/3J6dxJ

7. https://books2read.com/u/3yd90L

8. https://books2read.com/u/4ENaEA

9. https://books2read.com/u/4Nolg9

10. https://books2read.com/u/mvyGrX

11. https://books2read.com/u/3R0Aqj

The Frog Prince[13]
The Genie[14]
Peter & Pan[15]
The Fae Guardian[16]
The Dragon[17]

Monster Short Stories

Sniffed by the Dragon[18]
Deal with the Demon[19]
Servicing the Minotaur[20]
Bathing with the Akkorokamui[21]
Courted by El Sombrerón[22]
Saved by the Yeti[23]
Mated to a Vampire[24]
Bedding the God of Dreams[25]
Saved by the Grim Reaper[26]
Chased by the Werewolf[27]
Trapped with the Yeti[28]

---

12. https://books2read.com/u/bryN0w

13. https://books2read.com/u/bMzzY8

14. https://books2read.com/u/brexck

15. https://books2read.com/u/4AAqkp

16. https://books2read.com/u/38n6K6

17. https://books2read.com/u/br6YAW

18. https://books2read.com/u/boy8vV

19. https://books2read.com/links/ubl/3kYPzN

20. https://books2read.com/u/md1P5w

21. https://books2read.com/u/3LVqEX

22. https://books2read.com/u/38PLpB

23. https://books2read.com/u/bQj7VP

24. https://books2read.com/u/m2d8Y6

25. https://books2read.com/u/4ARgJo

26. https://books2read.com/u/bxrZZo

27. https://books2read.com/u/bzKW7Z

28. https://books2read.com/u/bopvPZ

Alien Erotica

Holiday Short Stories

29. https://books2read.com/u/3R0Lgv

30. https://books2read.com/u/m2qed1

31. https://books2read.com/u/3k6QvR

32. https://books2read.com/u/bxNkYD

33. https://books2read.com/u/bwB85Z

34. https://books2read.com/u/4DDDxQ

35. https://books2read.com/u/4NeVXz

36. https://books2read.com/u/bMzOl7

37. https://books2read.com/u/mZEGjR

38. https://books2read.com/u/ml8dvY

39. https://books2read.com/u/mvyO1J

40. https://books2read.com/u/bpYZxq

Sneak Peak of my next Erotic Fairytale: The Thief

"First rule of being a thief, princess, is not making a sound," Aladdin whispered in
my ear.
*A shiver passed through me as he slowly ground his hips against mine, pushing his
hard cock against my pussy. The footsteps passed us by and I had to hold back the
urge to bite him again. He lifted his hand from my mouth, lingering his fingers over
my lips. I opened my mouth, letting my tongue out to play, tasting him again.*
"I'm no princess," I growled against his fingers.
*My grip tightened around the crown, when I felt that he moved it higher above our
heads. He gently placed it on my head, startling me with the heavy weight of it.*
"But you look so good wearing a crown," he whispered before his mouth covered
mine.
*I moaned into the kiss, my hands grabbing his shoulders to keep me steady, my knife
loose in my hand, almost forgotten. He pushed me up against the wall, parting my
legs to make room for his hips. Before I knew what was happening, he was rubbing
his cock against my pussy, igniting pleasure as his tongue was playing with mine.
One of his hands slid in between us, underneath my robes, seeking out my aching
pussy. I really should tell him to stop, but it felt so good. When his hand reached my
wet pussy, he groaned into my mouth. The guards had passed us, but soon they
would discover that the crown was gone. His lips left mine as his fingers circled my
clit, making pleasure rise.*
"Such a little liar. You're sopping wet."
"Shut up," I growled.
The Thief: Erotic Fairytale Retelling - Coming Soon – January 2024

Printed in Great Britain
by Amazon

32379993R00040